THE
TATTLETALE

LYNN DOWNEY ILLUSTRATED BY **PAM PAPARONE**

HENRY HOLT AND COMPANY · NEW YORK

Wembly's brother, William, was a real tattletale.

One morning at breakfast, when Wembly
had a *terrible* itch in his snout, he scratched it.
   William told.
   "Oh dear, Wembly," his mama sighed.
"Scratching your snout is unsanitary. Please
go wash your hooves."

William snorted. Wembly
stuck his tongue out at him.

William told.
"Wembly," his mama sighed again.
"*Please* try to mind your manners."

Later, Grams and Grunt sent a crate of
Swamp Juice from Florida.
Mama stored the juice in the trough.

Wembly and William raced outside with the crate.

"I call first!" William cried.

But Wembly wasn't listening. He was busy admiring his next-door neighbor Iggy Hoggleswine (the toughest hog on the block) climb a very tall tree.

Wembly was afraid of heights. His hooves sweated and his head swooned just watching Iggy climb higher and higher.

In the crate William began his countdown. "One! Two . . ."

"Threeee!" Wembly tore his gaze from Iggy and jumped in behind William.

Z O O O O M—they zipped down the hill with Wembly whooping along.

"Hey! I called first!" William squealed when they came to a stop.

"Since when?" Wembly shot back.

William told.

"*Wembly*," his mama sighed for the third time. "That wasn't nice. What do you say to your brother?"

Wembly could think of lots of things he could say to his brother, but they would only get him into more trouble. So he apologized.

That night as they got ready
for bed, Wembly changed into his
Captain Sludge pajama shirt.

William grabbed the matching pants.
"Give them back!" Wembly snarled. "They're mine!"

"They're too small for you!" William snorted.

Wembly snatched the pants from William.
William told.

Mama marched in and seized the pajamas.
"Piggies! That's enough! From now on, you two
keep away from each other. Do you understand?"
"Yes, Mama," they both mumbled.

As soon as she left, Wembly drew a white line across the room.

"This is my half and that's yours," Wembly declared.

"Fine!" William snorted.
"Fine!" Wembly snorted back.

The next morning when William woke up, he heard a ruckus outside. From his half of the window he saw Wembly roaring with laughter as Iggy cannonballed—*kerrsplaaat!*— into an enormous mud puddle. Wembly joined in and got very dirty.

But William didn't tell. He just sat
and stared out the window.

Now Wembly was in pig heaven. Iggy
Hoggleswine was big. He was fearless.
And best of all, he didn't tattle.

William watched in horror as Wembly and Iggy
tore sheets off Mama's clothesline. They made
capes out of them and played Captain Sludge.

But William didn't tell.

They even scratched their snouts—
FIFTEEN TIMES!—and never washed
their hooves.

Still William did not tell.

Mama worried about William. "Why don't you go outside and play?"

William just shrugged.

She kissed his tuft. "Try and find something fun to do," Mama suggested.

But William didn't have any ideas.

Later that afternoon, Iggy and Wembly began making a tree fort. Iggy sat high on the branches assembling it, while Wembly handed him the wood. Iggy made a ladder to climb up. The final touch was a sign that read, NO TATTLETALES ALLOWED!

William felt sad and lonely.

Wembly began to climb the ladder v-e-r-y slowly. Suddenly he looked down—way, way down—and froze.

"I can't d-do it," he quivered. "It's t-too high."

"C'mon!" Iggy snorted. "What are you, scared?"

William watched his brother tremble. He remembered Wembly was afraid of heights. Without thinking he raced outside.

"I'll help you!" he shouted to his brother.

William started to go up the ladder but then
realized he wouldn't be able to get Wembly
down. Wembly was too heavy.

"I'll be right back!" William cried and flew into
the house.

"Awww—poor Wembly needs his wittle
bwother to save him!" Iggy clucked.

"You leave my brother out of this!" Wembly
said in a tiny voice. He *was* very scared.

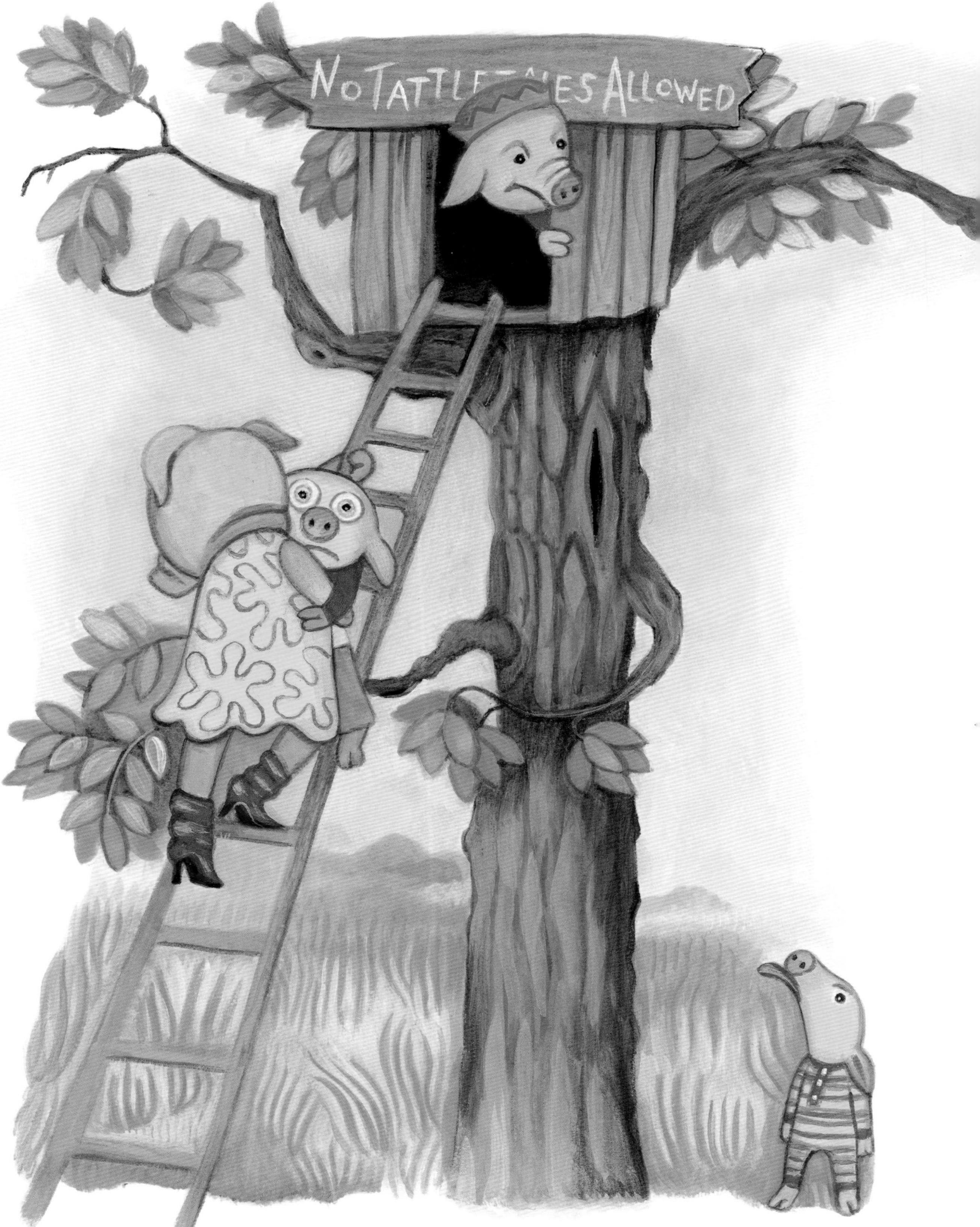
NO TATTLE
ES ALLOWED

Lickety-split, William returned with Mama.
She climbed up and brought Wembly down.
"Sissy!" Iggy hissed.
William stuck his tongue out at him before
Iggy disappeared inside the fort.

"Mama!" Wembly gasped when he was
safely on the ground. "You rescued me!"
"No," she replied. "William did."

Inside, Wembly erased the line in their room.
Wembly apologized for acting like a bully.
William apologized for tattling. They both promised
to be nicer to each other.

The next day Wembly surprised William
with a piggy-pup tent in the backyard.
The sign—
NO TATTLETALES ALLOWED—
was changed to:
NO BULLIES ALLOWED

"Thanks, Wembly! You're the best brother
in the whole world!" William exclaimed.

"No, you are," Wembly replied.

"No. You are!" William insisted.

"No! You are!" Wembly snorted.

"YOU ARE!" William snorted back.

"Okay, okay," Mama declared. "You BOTH are!"

And they couldn't have agreed more.

To Christy, for believing in my tales,
and to Amy for making it okay to tell them
—L. D.

For Sam
—P. P.

Henry Holt and Company, LLC, *Publishers since 1866*
175 Fifth Avenue, New York, New York 10010
www.henryholtchildrensbooks.com

Library of Congress Cataloging-in-Publication Data
Downey, Lynn.
The tattletale / Lynn Downey; illustrated by Pam Paparone.—1st ed.
p.   cm.
Summary: William the pig always tells their mother when his older brother Wembly does
something wrong, until he learns an important lesson about being a good brother.
ISBN-13: 978-0-8050-7152-8 / ISBN-10: 0-8050-7152-0
[1. Talebearing—Fiction. 2. Pigs—Fiction. 3. Brothers—Fiction.] I. Paparone, Pamela, ill. II. Title.
PZ7.D75915Tat 2006   [E]—dc22   2005020054

First Edition—2006 / Designed by Donna Mark and Amelia Anderson
The artist used acrylic on paper to create the illustrations for this book.
Printed in the United States of America on acid-free paper. ∞

1 3 5 7 9 10 8 6 4 2